A Note to Parents

Welcome to REAL KIDS READERS, a series of phonics-based books for children who are beginning to read. In the classroom, educators use phonics to teach children how to sound out unfamiliar words, providing a firm foundation for reading skills. At home, you can use REAL KIDS READERS to reinforce and build on that foundation, because the books follow the same basic phonic guidelines that children learn in school.

Of course the best way to help your child become a good reader is to make the experience fun—and REAL KIDS READERS do that, too. With their realistic story lines and lively characters, the books engage children's imaginations. With their clean design and sparkling photographs, they provide picture clues that help new readers decipher the text. The combination is sure to entertain young children and make them truly want to read.

REAL KIDS READERS have been developed at three distinct levels to make it easy for children to read at their own pace.

- LEVEL 1 is for children who are just beginning to read.
- LEVEL 2 is for children who can read with help.
- LEVEL 3 is for children who can read on their own.

A controlled vocabulary provides the framework at each level. Repetition, rhyme, and humor help increase word skills. Because children can understand the words and follow the stories, they quickly develop confidence. They go back to each book again and again, increasing their proficiency and sense of accomplishment, until they're ready to move on to the next level. The result is a rich and rewarding experience that will help them develop a lifelong love of reading.

For my mom, with love
—C. S.

For Destiny
—D. H.

Special thanks to Lands' End, Dodgeville, WI, for providing
Mom's bedding and Mike and Dave's pajamas.

Produced by DWAI / Seventeenth Street Productions, Inc.
Reading Specialist: Virginia Grant Clammer

Library of Congress Cataloging-in-Publication Data

Simon, Charnan.
  Surprise! / Charnan Simon ; photographs by Dorothy Handelman.
      p.   cm. — (Real kids readers. Level 2)
  Summary: When two brothers prepare a birthday surprise for their mother, her real surprise
comes when she sees the mess they have made.
  ISBN 0-7613-2068-7 (lib. bdg.). — ISBN 0-7613-2093-8 (pbk.)
  [1. Birthdays—Fiction. 2. Mothers and sons—Fiction. 3. Brothers—Fiction.] I. Handelman,
Dorothy, ill. II. Title. III. Series.
PZ7.S6035Su   1999
[E]—dc21
                                                                            98-52342
                                                                            CIP
                                                                            AC

pbk: 10 9 8 7 6 5 4 3 2 1
lib: 10 9 8 7 6 5 4 3 2 1

Surprise!

By **Charnan Simon**
Photographs by **Dorothy Handelman**

Dave and Mike got up
with the sun.
It was a good day.
It was a great day.
It was Mom's birthday!
Dave and Mike were glad.
There was just one thing wrong.
Dad was out of town.

Mom said, "I can wait for my party."
But Dave and Mike could not wait.
They wanted to make a surprise
for her.
"Go back to bed, Mom," said Dave.
"Yes," said Mike. "You look tired.
You should read and rest
for a while."

Mom went back to bed.
Dave and Mike went to work.
"Mom needs presents," said Mike.
"But we don't have any," said Dave.
"Then we will make some," said Mike.
So they did.

DISCARD

"What about birthday cards?"
asked Dave.
"We will make those too," said Mike.

The boys got out paper and paint.
They got out tape and glue.
They made the best cards ever.

"Now what?" asked Dave.
"How about a rose?" said Mike.
"Mom loves roses."
Dave went to get a vase.
Mike went to pick a rose.
Ouch!
He picked a thorn too!

13

Dave found a vase.
He filled it with water.
He filled it too full.
Oh, no!
Dave had a little spill.

"Let's make Mom a cake," said Mike.
"But we don't know how," said Dave.
"That's okay," said Mike.
"We will make a new kind of cake."

"Our cake looks good," said Dave.
"But it needs ice cream."
"Right," said Mike. "I'll get it."
"Let's use two kinds," said Dave.
"Good idea," said Mike.
"Let's make sure it's fresh," said Dave.
"Good idea," said Mike.

"Now we need snacks," said Mike.
"Lots and lots of snacks," said Dave.

The boys got out a tray.
They got out a plate and a glass.
They made lots and lots of snacks.

"Boys? Boys?"

It was Mom calling.

"May I get out of bed now?
I am all rested."

"NO!" the boys yelled back.

"You are still too tired," said Mike.

"We will come see you soon,"
added Dave.

"Quick!" said Mike.
"We have to hurry."

The boys got out ribbon.
They got out paper.
They worked fast!

At last the surprise was ready.
The boys sang all the way
to Mom's room.
"Happy birthday to you.
Happy birthday to you.
Happy birthday, dear Mom.
Happy birthday to you."

The text on the card reads: "Happy Birthday Mommy"

Mom was so surprised!
She loved her cards and presents.
She loved her rose.
She had never seen such good food.
"Please help me eat it," she said.
Mike and Dave were happy.
They had given Mom
a big surprise for her birthday.

A little later,
she got another big surprise.

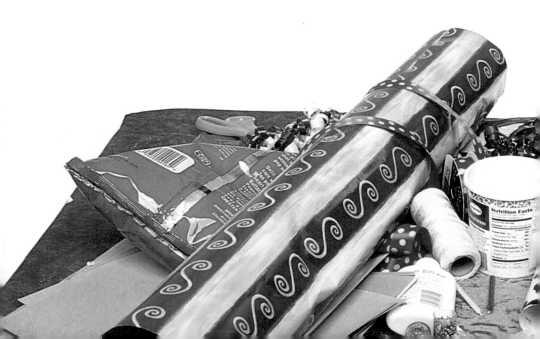

Phonic Guidelines

Use the following guidelines to help your child read the words in *Surprise!*

Short Vowels

When two consonants surround a vowel, the sound of the vowel is usually short. This means you pronounce *a* as in apple, *e* as in egg, *i* as in igloo, *o* as in octopus, and *u* as in umbrella. Short-vowel words in this story include: *big, but, can, dad, did, get, got, had, lots, Mom, not, sun, yes.*

Short-Vowel Words with Consonant Blends

When two or more different consonants are side by side, they usually blend to make a combined sound. In this story, short-vowel words with consonant blends include: *best, fast, glad, glass, help, just, last, sang, spill, still, went.*

Double Consonants

When two identical consonants appear side by side, one of them is silent. In this story, double consonants appear in the short-vowel words *full, will, yelled* and in the *all*-family word *all.*

R-Controlled Vowels

When a vowel is followed by the letter *r*, its sound is changed by the *r*. In this story, words with *r*-controlled vowels include: *cards, for, her, thorn.*

Long Vowel and Silent E

If a word has a vowel and ends with an *e*, usually the vowel is long and the *e* is silent. Long vowels are pronounced the same way as their alphabet names. In this story, words with a long vowel and silent *e* include: *cake, Dave, made, make, Mike, plate, rose, tape, vase.*

Double Vowels

When two vowels are side by side, usually the first vowel is long and the second vowel is silent. Double-vowel words in this story include: *cream, day, eat, may, need, paint, please, read, see, tray, wait, way.*

Diphthongs

Sometimes when two vowels (or a vowel and a consonant) are side by side, they combine to make a diphthong—a sound that is different from long or short vowel sounds. Diphthongs are: *au/aw, ew, oi/oy, ou/ow*. In this story, words with diphthongs include: *boys, found, how, new, now, ouch, out, town.*

Consonant Digraphs

Sometimes when two different consonants are side by side, they make a digraph that represents a single new sound. Consonant digraphs are: *ch, sh, th, wh*. In this story, words with digraphs include: *fresh, should, such, then, there, they, things, those, what, with.*

Silent Consonants

Sometimes when two different consonants appear side by side, one of them is silent. In this story, words with silent consonants include: *back, know, pick, right, snacks, wrong.*

Sight Words

Sight words are those words that a reader must learn to recognize immediately—by sight—instead of by sounding them out. They occur with high frequency in easy texts. Sight words not included in the above categories are: *a, and, at, be, come, could, go, good, have, he, I, it, little, look, loves, my, no, of, okay, one, our, said, so, some, soon, the, to, too, two, up, was, we, you.*